Darker Shade of Green

Darker Shade of Green © 2011 by Mickey Z.

Published by Raw Dog Screaming Press

Bowie, MD

First U.S. Edition

Cover Photo: Mickey Z.

Book Design: Jennifer Barnes

Printed in the United States of America

ISBN 978-1-935738-10-7

Library of Congress Control Number: 2011924030

www.RawDogScreaming.com

Darker Shade of Green

Mickey Z.

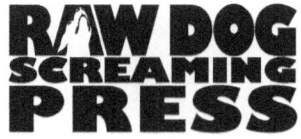

RAW DOG
SCREAMING
PRESS

Acknowledgments

With deep appreciation to Jennifer Barnes and John Lawson of Raw Dog Screaming Press (for all their support); David and Stephanie (for the blurbs); Michele, my Dad, the memory and influence of my Mom (for, well, everything), and to the enduring character of Allie Romano, who first came to me back in 1989 and has stayed by my side (in one form or another) ever since.

For AMA...

"I think we are in the midst of this period where we are committing suicide on the planet and everybody is just using up all of our natural resources like a bunch of insane people. That's what I worry about more than I worry about jazz."

—Sonny Rollins

"The earth is not dying. It is being killed, and the people killing it have names and addresses."

—Utah Phillips

It's never too late...

The dark green spray paint stained the sterile white East Side apartment building...the words threatening to reach out and strangle the passers-by while Allie Romano made his way down East 60th Street as the late afternoon rush began. His walk was reduced to nothing more than a shuffle and he appeared so much older than his years.

Why not? Had he not lived many times that amount in his fertile and vise-like mind? Surely Allie's physical deterioration was but a reflection of his mental prowess reaching its inescapable fruition.

Allie shuffled up to the green words, a can of paint in his right hand, virtually unnoticed. The callous breed of Upper East Side pedestrian was adept at giving him the feeling of being invisible. They did not see people like Allie; his was a strange anonymity.

Allie saw them, however. Allie Romano saw everything and felt everything. And, as he moved towards the words scrawled on the wall of the high-rise, Allie felt the world pressing against his chest, suffocating him.

Then, moving suddenly with the dexterity of an action painter, Allie splashed the can of red paint over the green words on the white wall. He didn't stop until the words were unreadable under the red deluge.

"You fool..." A nearby woman screamed at the disheveled homeless man as he tossed the empty paint can aside. "How dare you do that to the work of the East Side Prophet?"

"The East Side Prophet is a fraud," Allie countered, his voice barely above a whisper.

"You just destroyed poetry," a passing man joined in.

"Can't you appreciate art?" A second woman had positioned herself face-to-face with Allie as a crowd began to form. "Or are these messages too deep and too profound for you to understand?"

In a matter of minutes, an irate mob was converging on Allie Romano. The fans of the East Side Prophet were very mad, indeed.

"Don't you realize what you just did?" asked an angry young man with John Lennon-style glasses and a neat ponytail.

"I know all too well," Allie responded as he was shoved against the wall, his frail body weakening from the onslaught.

As the sound of sirens wailed in the distance, Allie was struck in the face by a large man and the feeding frenzy began.

Allie was buried under a barrage of kicks and punches from a mob thinking and acting as one.

Men and women in business suits—the same people who canonized the graffiti poetry of the East Side Prophet—were pounding on this weak man, punishing him for their misery.

Their faces clenched in expressions of profound fear, the well-heeled throng of upwardly mobile professionals drained the life from Alphonse "Allie" Romano. The East Side Prophet.

"From my close contact with authors and chess players, I have come to the personal conclusion that while all artists are not chess players, all chess players are artists."

—Marcel Duchamp

FADE IN

On a television tuned to an all-news channel. On screen is BART BLUM, a TV reporter with well-coiffed hair, blue contact lenses, and shiny white teeth. Behind him, we can see what appears to be a communication tower of some sort. It's clearly been knocked over.

> BART BLUM
> *(on TV)*
> Officials at the Department of
> Homeland Security would not
> comment yet but all indications
> are that this is a highly
> coordinated terror effort.
> Two hundred cell phone towers
> across America toppled at
> exactly 5:15—Eastern Time—this
> afternoon. Next to every downed
> tower was a chessboard with only
> the pawns set in place. Both
> black and white, the pawns were
> on the board without any other
> pieces. Local law enforcement
> authorities are calling it eco-
> terrorism. Local residents,
> however, are calling it a major
> nuisance.

CUT TO

                    LOCAL WOMAN
                      (on TV)
My cell phone is totally useless
now and I don't even have a home
phone anymore. Who does? I hope
these animals are caught and put
away for a long time. They're
saying this is a political act
but what the heck is political
about cell phones?

CUT TO

One of Allie's first posts on Craigslist as the so-called "Internet Insurgent":

Every time a cell phone rings, we should focus on these six simple words: The Democratic Republic of the Congo. We'd do that because one of the primary components of cell phone circuitry is a metallic ore called Columbite-Tantalite—or "coltan." Eighty percent of the world's known coltan can be found in the African nation of The Democratic Republic of the Congo (or DRC), which just so happens to be embroiled in a brutal (even by current standards) civil war since the pre-cell phone days of 1994. Over time, all sides in the unrelenting struggles adroitly began using the mining and sale of coltan not only to nourish the West's seemingly insatiable cell phone addiction, but also to fund their inexorable mayhem.

Civilian deaths in the DRC during this time—mostly from war-related disease and malnutrition—are estimated not in the hundreds, thousands, or tens of thousands, but rather in the millions...making it the world's deadliest military conflict since the Second World War.

And it gets worse. Just ask an Eastern Lowland Gorilla, the world's largest primate, found almost exclusively in the DRC. According to *National Geographic*: "Following a decade of civil war in the Democratic Republic of the Congo, new estimates suggest that the number of eastern lowland gorillas may have plummeted by 70 percent. Conflict, illegal mining for a mineral used for electronic-device components, and the growing bush-meat trade have all taken their toll." The UN Environment Program has reported that the number of eastern lowland gorillas in eight DRC national parks has subsequently declined by 90 percent.

We can only hope that some enterprising soul has already recorded the eastern lowland gorilla's call so it can be used as a ring tone long after they're gone.

Excerpt from the Pawns' press release, claiming responsibility for Operation Can-You-Hear-Me-Now:

There are 77,000 radio-transmission towers higher than 199 feet in the U.S. and nearly 200 million birds collide fatally with these towers per year. Add in 175,000 cell phone towers and the number of dead birds approaches a half-billion annually.

Allie Romano's Favorite Movie:

The Battle of Algiers

JT's Favorite Movie:

V for Vendetta

❧

YOUR NARRATOR: *It wasn't long after the downed cell phone towers event that the media caught on to a very juicy angle: the young reclusive American chess champion James Tanger—a.k.a. Jimmy T.—was involved in a big way. Clever headlines called for "checkmate" and their use of the term "endgame" lacked any awareness of what The Pawns were up to. For writers like me, it all made perfect sense. The connections were transparent...and that's why I was allowed to conduct an e-mail interview with Jimmy T. I started by asking him if he preferred "JT" now.*

JT: It's up to you. It started as James Tanger, then Jimmy T. and these days, just JT. You know, covert action and all.

How did your group choose the name "Pawns"?

JT: They left it up to me. It's more a tribute to Allie than to chess. I was gonna use "Allies" but it seemed too obvious and it's too linked to the so-called Good War.

Allie was dead-on with how the corporate media would cover The Pawns, by the way. I remember him telling me this: "Whether you label them liberal or conservative, most major media outlets are large corporations owned by or aligned with even larger corporations, and they share a common goal: to make a profit by selling a product—an affluent audience—to a given market: advertisers. Therefore, we shouldn't find it too shocking that the image of the world being presented by a corporate-owned press very much reflects the biased interests of the elite players involved in this sordid little love triangle. That's why every major daily newspaper has a business section, but not a labor section. Why at least once a week those same newspapers run an automobile section, but no bicycle section. This is why when the Dow Jones Industrial Average drops, it makes headlines. But if the global infant mortality rate rises, it's questionable if it will even make the papers—and if it does, it'll be buried on page 23. In other words, if you created a blueprint for an apparatus that utterly erased critical thought, you could make none more efficient than the American corporate media."

Wait...who's Allie?

JT: The Pawns guidebook is basically his words. Five mini-chapters based on what I learned from Alphonse Romano.

Chapter I from *The Rise of the Pawns*:

How to be a good organizer

a) Spend some time thinking about trees

b) Imagine what clear cutting looks like, sounds like, and feels like

c) Recognize that 80% of the world's forests are gone

d) Be a good organizer

But who's Allie?

JT: He's the reason I'm the American chess champion. He's the reason I'm a Pawn. He's the reason you're interviewing me.

The paper sign read:

ALL BOOKS: $3.00

Below that, the quiet homeless man in the tattered cap had meticulously scrawled these words:

PLAY THE CHESS MASTER FOR $5.00.
IF YOU WIN, YOU GET $10.00.
A DRAW GETS YOUR MONEY BACK.

JT: I was only twelve years old when I stared long and hard at that hand-written sign. It was as if I had reached my launching pad. Lined up on the table were hardcover books—all the latest best sellers—in *perfect* condition.

Next to them sat an old chess set with the pieces set up, ready to do battle. It's the only chessboard I still own today. The man sitting behind this display showed utter indifference to me, to everyone for that matter. He was Alphonse "Allie" Romano; former child prodigy and one of New York's ever-expanding legions of homeless people.

From the National Coalition for the Homeless

AGE

In 2003, children under the age of 18 accounted for 39% of the homeless population; 42% of these children were under the age of five (National Law Center on Homelessness and Poverty, 2004). This same study found that unaccompanied minors comprised 5% of the urban homeless population. However, in other cities and especially in rural areas, the numbers of children experiencing homelessness are much higher. According to the National Law Center on Homelessness and Poverty, in 2004, 25% of homeless were ages 25 to 34; the same study found percentages of homeless persons aged 55 to 64 at 6%.

GENDER

Most studies show that single homeless adults are more likely to be male than female. In 2007, a survey by the U.S. Conference of Mayors found that of the population surveyed 35% of the homeless people who are members of households with children are male while 65% of these people are females. However, 67.5% of the single homeless population are males, and it is this single population that makes up 76% of the homeless populations surveyed (U.S. Conference of Mayors, 2007).

JT: Allie read from a dog-eared and worn copy of *The Air-Conditioned Nightmare* by Henry Miller that stood in stark contrast to the gleaming tomes on his table. He gazed almost lovingly at the pages, his deep blue eyes seemed to devour the words, and only on occasion, did he glanced up to check if he had a customer.

I tried to make eye contact, but Allie ignored his small admirer.

"I'd like to play you in chess, sir."

Allie let his eyes rise from the page to examine my earnest expression. His head did not move, he merely allowed his deeply sunken eyes to move upward like rippling, bottomless pools of shocking blue water. He told me later that I seemed innocent and fresh. When Allie saw the wad of bills in my tiny hand, he reluctantly nodded.

Another post by the Internet Insurgent:

William Burroughs once wrote about how we humans—like the bull in a bullfight—tend to focus on the elusive red cape instead of the matador. Indeed, we are all-too-easily distracted from real targets by an attractive image or illusion.

Of course, some bulls see right through the red cape, uh, bullshit...and quite justifiably introduce the matador to the business end of their horns. Before you mistake that for a lesson and/or inspiration, don't forget that such bulls are promptly killed while the matador is mourned as a brave hero.

Here's my question: If every bull in every bullfight were to gore every matador, how long would it be before bullfights were a thing of the past?

JT: I began with a Queen's pawn opening that, incongruously, I would never use again in my many future tournament wins. Allie appeared to be vaguely distracted until he noticed that I had a clear advantage. My precocious strategy was simple, but effective. Squinting his eyes in disdain, Allie began to play for the draw.

I sensed surrender and moved in for the kill, offering my hand to the homeless man. Allie resigned after 47 moves. I collected his $5.00, but insisted on a "double or nothing" rematch. Allie obliged by promptly whipping me five consecutive times until he had to demand that I leave him alone.

"I want to stay here with you, sir. It's *you* that I came looking for."

Allie winced, ignoring his "fan." I just grinned, pulled up a milk crate, and joined Allie next to the books.

"Where do you get all these brand new books, sir?"

"Call me Alphonse." His voice was barely above a whisper...the kind of voice that made you lean in close just to hear.

"Where do you get these books, Alphonse? And how can you sell them so cheaply?

He did not appear to hear these queries. His shrugs and changing facial expressions gave me the impression that Allie was engaged in an internal dialogue. I smiled and went about watching and listening to a songbird in a nearby tree, marveling at how the passing lunchtime crowd, in all their bustling insanity, did not even notice my feathered friend.

25

Perhaps, I wondered to myself, if I dropped a few coins on the sidewalk these poor misguided souls would stop and look. How sad: in tune with the sound of money, oblivious to the wonders of nature.

Money doesn't talk, it swears

A 2007 Gallup poll found 72% of respondents with incomes of at least $75,000 reported being very satisfied with their personal life, while only 36% of those with an annual income of $30,000 or less said the same.

Why has this never been mentioned in any of your official chess biographies?

JT: I chose to wait. My family was mortified so I never had to worry about any of them bringing it up. Now, I'm much more than a chess player, so this story must be told.

What are you, besides a chess player?

JT: (*chuckles*) I like to think of myself as an "event planner" now.

What events are you planning?

JT: We'll get to that soon enough. For now, I need to explain Allie's role in all this.

"Let's cut out the transcendental twaddle when the whole thing is as plain as a sock on the jaw."

—Ludwig Wittgenstein

❦

JT: By the end of the day, I had succeeded in relaying my brief life story to my new homeless companion: born to a hugely rich Boston developer, raised by maids and nannies, neglected by my parents, and driven to running away.

Allie mocked this as nothing more than a hollow gesture aimed at getting attention. I didn't mind this assessment in the least and I did not defend myself. Allie noted this with some amusement.

Throughout the day, I watched as Allie easily defeated every chess challenger. His style was ruthless, and I studied each move, keeping notations in a small notebook Allie gave me.

It was while thumbing through this notebook that I first realized that this disheveled, homeless chess master was "The Spray Can Prophet." My eyes bulged when I saw such entries as:

**All roads lead
to no where**

But they are always filled

JT: All one had to do was read the daily newspaper articles and blog posts on the graffiti poet currently holding the city under his spell. Maxims, poems, and one-liners scrawled in dark green paint on New York's tenements and subway walls, all focusing on the absurdity of living in a corporate-run society. Some even were linking the graffiti with the sudden appearance of very radical posts in the "political" section on Craigslist...posts soon attributed to the "Internet Insurgent."

I was overflowing with excitement. Throughout my young life, I dreamt of being a writer and becoming a chess master. My parents ignored these interests, my peers mocked me, and I was forced into a self-imposed isolation.

How I yearned to speak out. I saw my frustrating situation as typical of life. Profound insight for a twelve-year-old, perhaps, but my youthful mind was fertile and filled with budding cynicism.

Now I had met Allie Romano. I didn't know why I escaped to New York, but I suddenly felt confident about my decision. Here I was, sitting next to a man with phenomenal chess skill, a genius who held the city captive by his words, and—most importantly—a man who was indifferent to it all. He was focused on much bigger issues.

Chapter II from *The Rise of the Pawns*:

How to find like-minded comrades

a) Go to the beach

b) Smell the salty air and listen to the waves

c) Recognize that 90% of the large fish in the ocean are gone

d) Find like-minded comrades

JT: I asked him, "Where will you sleep tonight?"

Allie sensed what I was getting at and did not waste his time trying to talk his obstinate protégé out of joining him. His home was a beaten-down shack at the mouth of the 59th Street Bridge.

Cars and trucks streamed on and off the bridge all day and night, but Allie no longer saw or heard them. It wasn't as easy for me to sleep under these conditions. My real home was a mansion. My bed was fit for a prince. Still, I somehow felt safe next to Allie, and I eventually gave way to dreams of chess, graffiti poems, and a dangerous new future.

More from the Internet Insurgent:

When you flick on a light switch, you are playing your role in the creation of valley fills. Here's how one of the big green groups begins its discussion of mountaintop removal mining: "In places like Appalachia, mining companies blow the tops off mountains to reach a thin seam of coal and then, to minimize waste disposal costs, dump millions of tons of waste rock into the valleys below, causing permanent damage to the ecosystem and landscape."

That is a valley fill.

Electricity—and all of industrial culture—comes at a very high price and the bill is overdue.

❧

JT: As if I had wished the rain upon the city, a torrential downpour kept me and Allie in the shack for the entire next day. I used this opportunity to get my mentor to work on my chess skills. I marveled at his encyclopedic knowledge of endgame variations.

"The true fighter proves his mettle in the endgame," Allie told me. "Develop a solid opening repertoire, cultivate the patience needed for the middle game, but let your natural ability and desire lead you through the endgame."

We ate some food that Allie bought with his book money, we played chess, and we read. Still, I felt as if I'd explode from all the questions I wanted my homeless mentor to answer.

"Why don't you compete in chess tournaments?"

"Why do you live here?"

"Are you the Spray Can Prophet?"

"Where do you get all these brand new books?"

"It's a primitive scam," replied Allie, choosing to respond only to my last question. "I watch for moving vans, get the name and address of the people who are moving, and sign them up to The Book of the Month Club. I watch for the delivery and take the books. Quite unimpressive, yet it serves my meager purposes."

"That's great! I can help you! I'll go around looking for moving vans! I'll do that for you, Alphonse!"

Allie laid back and fell asleep. Undaunted, I replayed our last chess game, searching for new combinations. The rain continued into the night, keeping me off the streets.

Herbert Mercury, the private detective hired by my father to find his prodigal son, would have never thought to look inside the shanty that a homeless prophet called home.

Mercury doubted that I was in the Big Apple, but Dad felt sure that I would seek out a large metropolis. He warned Herbert Mercury to watch the chess clubs closely. So, the obese private dick enjoyed the big payday while it lasted.

Convinced that his juvenile guest was fast asleep, Allie went out later that night when the rain had cleared. I slipped out after him, tailing my hero in and out of the towering Manhattan shadows. Allie carried a small can of green paint and a brush. He didn't use spray paint, contrary to one of the media nicknames.

Rust Oleum Textured Spray Paint (aerosol)

Warnings:

Extremely flammable liquid and vapors

Vapors may cause flash fire

Contents under pressure

Contains Acetone and Xylene. Vapor harmful. May affect brain or nervous system causing dizziness, headache or nausea. Causes eye, skin, nose and throat irritation. Harmful if swallowed.

Reports have associated repeated and prolonged occupational overexposure to solvents with premature brain and nervous system damage. Do not breathe vapors, spray mist, sanding dust or overspray. To avoid breathing vapors or spray mist, open windows and doors or use other means to ensure fresh air entry during application or drying. If you experience eye watering, headaches or dizziness, increase fresh air or wear respiratory protection or leave area. Follow respirator manufacturer's directions for respirator use. Avoid contact with eyes, skin and clothing. Vapors may ignite explosively. Keep away from heat, sparks and flame. Extinguish all flames and pilot lights, and turn off stoves, heaters, electric motors and other sources of ignition during use and until all vapors are gone. Do not smoke. Use only with adequate ventilation. Prevent build-up of vapors by opening all windows and doors to achieve cross-ventilation. Do not expose to heat or store at temperatures above 120 degrees F. Exposure to heat or prolonged exposure to sun may cause bursting. Do not puncture or incinerate container. Replace cap after each use. This product contains chemicals known to cause cancer and birth defects or other reproductive harm.

Excerpt from the script I'm writing about Allie and JT:

FADE IN

On Allie and JT walking slowly through Manhattan's Upper East Side. Rush hour has passed and dusk has calmed the streets. The boy trails his hero in and out of the towering Manhattan shadows.

Allie carries a small can of green paint and a brush. He reaches into his coat pocket and produces a few packages of crackers, which he crumbles and tosses to a bunch of birds: pigeons, sparrows, and starlings.

                    ALLIE
          As many as 80 million birds are
          killed each year by collisions
          with plate glass windows.
          Another 60 to 80 million birds
          are killed each year by motor
          vehicles. 120 million birds are
          murdered by hunters each year.
          Domestic cats kill about 4
          million birds each day in North
          America alone. There are 77,000
          radio-transmission towers higher
          than 199 feet in the U.S. and
          nearly 200 million birds collide

fatally with these towers per
year. Add in 175,000 cell phone
towers and the number of dead
birds approaches a half-billion
annually.

JT stares at the birds, a tear sliding down
his face.

> JT
>
> Wow...I...

> ALLIE
>
> Then, of course, you have
> habitat loss, environmental
> toxins, introduced diseases,
> and the biggest bird killer of
> all: the meat-based diet. For
> example, every day, 23 million
> chickens are killed in the
> U.S. for food. That's 269 dead
> chickens per second.

> JT
>
> Everyone hates pigeons but I
> kinda like them.

> ALLIE
>
> *Columba livia*, a.k.a. Rock
> Pigeon. I remember when the
> mayor said, "We do have a lot
> of pigeons and they do tend to

foul a lot of our areas." (beat)
Just for the hell of it, let's
replace the word "pigeons" with
the word "corporations" in that
statement. How about if we just
insert "humans"?

                    JT
Why are pigeons so hated,
Alphonse?

                  ALLIE
For some, the feral pigeon could
be viewed as a nuisance. But
in all the thousands of years
Columba livia have dwelled on this
planet, did any of them ever
feel the need to invent, say,
nuclear weapons? No Rock Dove
created pesticides, napalm,
Agent Orange, or the internal
combustion engine; you can't
blame cigarettes, greenhouse
gases, hydroelectric dams,
waterboarding, or mercury-
laced vaccinations on a
pigeon; and rest assured no
non-human conjured up zoos,
animal experimentation, factory
farming, or the rodeo.

JT: Allie loved birds and I remember one of my favorite parables of his. He told me about the European house sparrow. In 1853, the future founders of the Brooklyn Botanic Garden set free several pairs of the previously unknown European house sparrow inside Brooklyn's Greenwood Cemetery. By picking the hayseeds out of horse droppings, the tiny birds thrived and are now one of the nation's most ubiquitous creatures.

Then he told me about the Dusky Seaside sparrow. Once found mainly on Florida's Merritt Island, the dusky seaside sparrow had its salt marsh habitat sprayed with DDT and cleared so it could be taken over by the space program. The last Dusky died in 1987.

Then he asked me this question:

Will you allow them to poison you into extinction or will you survive by finding the hayseeds amidst the horseshit?

From Allie's notebook:

They ask me why I can't be normal. What's normal?

Normal means New Hampshire license plates bear the words "Live free or die"

Normal means New Hampshire license plates are manufactured by prisoners

❧

JT: You asked earlier about what events The Pawns have in mind. Well, consider this: As I sit in New York City writing this, I am reminded that the Indian Point nuclear reactor (one of over a hundred such reactors in the U.S.) is only *thirty-five miles* from the center of Manhattan and, as Helen Caldicott describes, "A meltdown would...[trap] millions of people in a radioactive hell, unable to escape, dying within forty-eight hours of acute radiation illness. Such an event is not unlikely according to the Nuclear Regulatory Commission, because this reactor is plagued with safety problems.

Why am I telling you this? Well, it's time we ask ourselves what we fear most?

And, as you see it, what do we fear most?

JT: Our acquiescence in a disturbingly broad range of areas—access to health care, tolerance for voting irregularities, stomaching the groupthink behind saluting a flag, etc. etc. etc.—appears to have no limits.

Americans love to talk the talk about being fearless and tough but when ordered to remove our shoes before going through airport security, it's "yes sir" all the way.

We know things have passed the proverbial tipping point and that immediate action is 100% needed *and* justified, but we're far too spineless to do anything that might get us in trouble.

Somehow, it's more terrifying for any of us to face down a cop than it is to contemplate the total destruction of our earthly ecosystem. Perhaps, if we were more in touch with the pain of others, we'd be better activists.

Another excerpt from my unproduced screenplay:

DISS TO

Allie and JT inside the shack: sitting across from each other, staring silently at the pieces on a chessboard. Judging from the positions, they are in the endgame.

Suddenly, they are jolted by the SOUND of screeching tires. Allie is snapped from his chess trance as he jumps up to move to the door and have a look.

CUT TO

ALLIE'S POV: A CROWD is gathering around a white SUV. A YOUNG BOY has been hit. There's blood everyone. SCREAMS are heard but the boy is silent.

                        JT
                      (O/S)
        What is it, Alphonse?

CUT TO

Allie's face. He is crying. Weeping.

                    ALLIE
      During the 40 days of the first
      Gulf War, 146 Americans died
      keeping the world safe for
      petroleum while back here in the
      homeland, 4900 Americans died in
      motor vehicle accidents.

JT, by now, is looking out the door, too. He begins crying as he reaches up to hold Allie's hand.

                    JT
      Is he gonna die?

                    ALLIE
      Perhaps now. Perhaps later.
      We're all doomed, my friend,
      unless someone fights back.
      (looks at JT) They'll poison us or
      imprison us or run us down with
      their machines if we don't fight
      so...

                    JT
                (overlapping)
      ...what have we got to lose by
      fighting?

Allie wipes his face and nods. He and JT walk slowly toward the accident scene as an ambulance siren ECHOES in the distance.

FADE OUT

JT: You've got me jumping way ahead. I wanna go back to that night I followed Allie all over the East Side until he found the right spot for his graffiti.

He surveyed many walls before settling on those of The Vertical Club, a vast Upper East Side health club. Moving quicker than I had ever seen him move, Allie dashed on the paint like an abstract expressionist and hastily exited. I stood back for a second to appraise the words:

> **Life's parade marches
> on didn't you hear
> the starting gun?**

JT: Quickly, I dashed back to the shack to avoid being discovered. Allie entered and began to read. *Pacifism as Pathology* by Ward Churchill, I believe it was. Oh, how I tried to stay awake to watch him, but my second day as a homeless New Yorker had exhausted me, and I was soon asleep.

The next day, Allie sat impassively behind his chessboard while a young, upwardly mobile man attempted to salvage his pride by trading queens. Allie's next move brought the man to the brink of defeat, and he opted for resignation over checkmate. I arrived at that point.

"What a day, Alphonse. I spent three hours looking for moving vans, and I got four addresses for you."

"A fruitful morning."

"Plus, I fell in love today. This girl on the train just stopped me in my tracks."

"Love?"

"She was a bit old for me. At least twenty. But I couldn't take my eyes off of her. Long black hair...and she was wearing a hat."

"Intriguing."

"You probably think I'm exaggerating when I say I fell in love, but it wasn't immediate."

"I'm sure at least three minutes passed."

"A little more than that. She was reading *The World According to Garp*, a book I happen to like. So, when this seat opens up, she sits down. I stood next to her and saw she was up to the part where Garp's little boy dies in the car accident. What's his name again?"

"Walt."

"Yeah, Walt. She gets to this part and I notice that my dream girl is crying. Can you believe it?"

"You have no reason to lie."

"Well, this really touched me. So, when it reached my stop, I reached over and brushed away one tear. She looked up at me kinda surprised. You know what I told her right before I got off?"

"I couldn't imagine."

"I said, 'You are so lucky to have such sensitivity. Stay that way.'

Then I kissed my finger because it had her tear on it, and I walked right off the train. Whaddya think?"

"How would you like to do the honors at the chessboard today?"

Another entry from the Internet Insurgent:

The world's worst polluter is not your cousin who refuses to recycle or the co-worker who drives a gas guzzler or that guy down the block who simply will not try CFL bulbs. "The U.S. Department of Defense is the largest polluter in the world, producing more hazardous waste than the five largest U.S. chemical companies combined.

Pesticides, defoliants like Agent Orange, solvents, petroleum, lead, mercury, and depleted uranium are among the many deadly substances used by the military.

What does this mean for us? To start with, it can help illustrate how to best foment a green revolution.

"Even if every single person in the United States were to change all their light-bulbs to fluorescent, cut the amount they drive in half, recycle half of their household waste, inflate their tire pressure to increase gas mileage, use low flow shower heads and wash clothes in lower temperature water, adjust their thermostats two degrees up or down depending on the season, and plant a tree, it would result in a one time, 21% reduction in carbon emissions."

For those of you scoring at home, that's a one time, 21% reduction in carbon emissions. We compost, we drive hybrids, we bring our own bag to the market but meanwhile, the U.S. military and its fellow polluters—trans-national corporations—treat the planet like it's a porta-potty...with little or no opposition from the general population. In fact, the military typically enjoys unconditional support even from those who identify as "anti-war."

Keep this in mind the next time you hear the phrase "war on terror": Our tax dollars are subsidizing a global eco-terror campaign and all the recycled toilet paper in the world ain't gonna change that.

JT: "Not bad, huh, Alphonse? I only lost one with three draws, and I must've played at least twenty-five games."

"It just goes to show how easy it is to get people to give their money away," Allie remarked as he shared his dinner with me back at the hovel. The weather had taken a turn for the worst, and Allie and his new apprentice huddled together for warmth.

Chapter III from *The Rise of the Pawns*:

How to plan a protest

a) *200,000 acres of rain forest are destroyed each day. Picture a planet devoid of rain forests. Picture a human body without lungs.*

b) *A woman is raped every 46 seconds in America. Visualize the terror and trauma of these experiences.*

c) *29,158 children under the age of five die from preventable causes each day. Imagine the feelings of grief, sorrow, and loss.*

d) Plan a protest.

When was the last time you played chess?

JT: Truth be told, I used to play online a lot...under assumed names. Usually as "Allie" or "Alphonse." It's a form of relaxation to play anonymously and see how surprised the other players are when they are thoroughly dismantled.

When was the last time you did that?

JT: It's been a little while because one of the players somehow figured out whom he was playing and dig this: he wanted to join The Pawns. He wanted to send me money for "the cause" and offer me a place to stay.

How did he realize it was you?

JT: Good question. But since all this started, I sometimes feel like Tyler Durden. People I don't even know greet me like a long-lost friend—both online and in person.

There are more pawns out there than the kings and queens realize.

JT: There always are but numbers mean nothing without action.

Did you take that guy up on his offer?

JT: Which guy?

The chess player who wanted to join The Pawns and hide you out.

JT: No way. It's the oldest cop trick in the book.

A poem from the Internet Insurgent:

game plan

*your heart
has windows
...open them*

*talk to your
neighbors*

*kill the cop
inside you
(but not the judge)*

*connect your freedom
to everyone else's
freedom*

*don't wait for death
to experience heaven*

JT: Anyway, that evening—the night after I snuck around to watch Allie—he did not wait for me to follow him on his graffiti-poetry trek. Somehow, he knew that I saw the previous night's trip, and he merely told me to get my jacket and follow him.

It was intoxicating for me to be out so late at night especially since Allie was unable to decide on a site for his words. At least two hours passed before he found a suitable setting.

This entire time period Allie spent answering my innocent query; his whispery voice was like the sound of an ancient spirit talking.

"Alphonse, why do you do this instead of working and getting married and all that?

"This country is built on the principle of maintaining the proverbial status quo," he began. "A vast, comprehensive, and inhuman system has been implemented to ward off challenges to this status quo. Acceptance of this ever-growing system has slowly become an almost inbred characteristic of Americans. Hence, even hinting at chinks in the armor is greeted with vehement resistance, even from the misguided oppressed themselves. The fervor of this resistance is tantamount to self-defense.

"For years, I've heard people question my sanity after hearing my thoughts on the system. They wonder if I really believe this to be true. It hardly matters. The system exists with or without our belief. I've chosen to see it for what it is. Perhaps I'd be wiser to simply conform, but my mind will not let me.

"Fighting the proverbial system can give one a great feeling of self-respect but it will surely lead to your destruction. *All paths of glory lead but to the grave.* The path of challenging the system is merely a shortcut."

As Allie completed his dissertation, I stepped back to take in his painted words before we headed back to our shack:

when wall street coughs,
governments tumble
when infant mortality rises,
mr. dow jones yawns

From Allie's notebook:

Normal means land mines, factory farming, and the death penalty

It means racial profiling and the shooting of abortion doctors

Normal means gay bashing and it means "illegal" is a noun

It means pesticide, homicide, suicide, genocide

JT told me about the time he and Allie walked through Times Square and saw Spray Can Prophet copycat graffiti near the military recruiting station:

don't
support
the
troops

JT: Allie really smirked at the dark green words. Not only was he inspiring others to action but he was also provoking such a decidedly non-mainstream sentiment. I asked him if it made sense for an anti-war activist to support "our" troops and he began a powerful critique of America's military fetish. I'm not sure if Allie knew a Marine recruiter was listening but I didn't see the guy until he interjected a comment.

Here's a rough idea of how that conversation went:

ALLIE: For some, the phrase "support our troops" is merely a euphemism for: support the policies that put the troops there in the first place. For others—particularly on the Left—it is a safe way to avoid taking an unqualified stand against this war and *all* war. Many who passionately identify as "anti-war" will just as passionately defend the troops-no questions asked—and the excuse making typically falls into three categories: They were just following orders, it's a "poverty draft," and the troops are fighting for our freedom.

(That's when the Marine stepped out of the doorway and added his two cents. I jumped out of my skin. Allie just sighed.)

RECRUITER: While you stand here polluting this young man's mind, those brave men and women are putting their asses on the line to fight for your freedom to spew your anti-American garbage.

ALLIE: *Bullshit.*

RECRUITER: Excuse me?

ALLIE: I say bullshit.

RECRUITER: You can't tell me—

ALLIE: The troops in Iraq and Afghanistan are not fighting for my freedom. They are fighting to keep the world safe for petroleum. If anything, since 9/11, our freedom has been slowly eroded and the presence of the U.S. military in Iraq and Afghanistan makes it harder for anyone to speak up in dissent.

RECRUITER: You're doing it now, ain't ya?

ALLIE: If I said the same thing while walking through an airport—especially near the security area—I'd likely be detained, maybe arrested.

RECRUITER: No one will arrest you, my friend. Go ahead, tell me more. Tell me about the following orders part.

ALLIE: We are not and never will be friends. *(pause)* The only following orders excuse has no legal foundation. For example, Principle IV of the Nuremberg Tribunal states: "The fact that a person acted pursuant to order of his government or of a superior does not relieve him from responsibility under international law provided a moral choice was in fact possible to him." Besides this, it can be easily posited that "only following orders" also has no moral footing. Of course, the facile example would be Nazi Germany. Yet, somehow, today's volunteer warriors are given a free pass because they didn't give the orders in an illegal war and occupation. This is not only illegal and immoral; it also lacks any radical credibility. Somehow, individuals and groups can stand tall against war and military intervention but refuse to shine a light on those who choose and get paid to fight. Nowhere else in the realm of activism does such a paradox exist.

RECRUITER: Wait, activism?

ALLIE: Yes, do you actually think I'm addressing my thoughts to people like you? No, I'd rather try to sway those who at least think they are anti-war.

RECRUITER: I'm a lost cause, huh?

ALLIE: *(ignoring the wisecrack)* Consider the animal rights activists struggling to end the morally indefensible and scientifically fraudulent enterprise of animal experimentation. Can they expose the corporations and academic institutions but somehow "support" the actual scientists performing the lab experiments? Surely, they are "just doing their job" and "following orders." How about those fighting to end unfair labor practices? Is it acceptable to call out the CEOs of Nike and The Gap but hang yellow ribbons for those who handle day-to-day operations of a sweatshop in, say, Vietnam? These men and women are just as "stuck in a bad situation" as any grunt in Iraq or Afghanistan.

RECRUITER: We give those grunts training and a job? Do you even know what a job is?

ALLIE: Ah yes, here comes the "poverty draft" excuse. These poor souls have to enlist because they don't have any economic options, right? America is certainly an unjust economic society and this would be a compelling argument...if it were true. But a study found that wartime recruits since 1999 are comparable to the youth population on the whole, except that they are on average a bit wealthier, much more likely to have graduated from high school and more rural than their civilian peers. It also found that youths from wealthy American ZIP codes are volunteering in ever higher numbers while enlistees from the poorest fifth of American neighborhoods fell nearly a full percentage point over the last two years, to 13.7 percent."

RECRUITER: Anyone can cite statis—

ALLIE: For the sake of argument, let's say those numbers are inaccurate and let's say that most of today's enlistees volunteer because they lack almost any other economic options. What I'm wondering is this: Would this same economic excuse hold water for those who opt to become gang members for the same exact reason? A poor black kid "enlists" in the Crips, a poverty-stricken Hispanic "enlists" in the Latin Kings...for that matter: an uneducated Italian kid in Bensonhurst "enlists" in the Mafia. These kids are also faced with a stark choice—being poor or choosing a uniform—but no one hangs yellow ribbons for them, no one makes excuses for them.

This is when the recruiter tried a different tack.

RECRUITER: *(to me)* Why aren't you in school, young man? Who is this filthy man to you? Are you safe?

ALLIE: There are two major differences between those gang members and the men and women who volunteer to join the U.S. military: The U.S. military is far more dangerous than any gang or Mafia family and the U.S. military is considered legal.

This is when the recruiter's face turned red in rage and he moved toward Allie. I surprised myself by punching him directly in the balls with all my might. I screamed "fuck you" as I did. He made an odd sound and dropped to the sidewalk.

Allie did not seem shocked by my outburst as he spit on the sidewalk near the fallen hero.

ALLIE: This is why I don't usually debate lost causes. For me now, it's all about creating or finding a softer place to land.

We ran off and I could've sworn Allie was giggling...

Another communiqué from the Internet Insurgent:

Embrace not the corporate sanctioned standard American diet; go vegan, organic, and local. Be warned: what you own ends up owning you; say no to conspicuous consumption. Opt for two wheels, not four; bid a fond farewell to your internal combustion engine. Under no circumstances should you cast a vote for either a Democrat or a Republican; these are but two wings on one corporate party. Never, ever, ever trust a liberal (on *anything*). Reject both war *and* its warriors; offer not your support to those who volunteer to wage war. Reach out for your television remote and boldly press "off" (toss the cell phone, too). 6.6 billion miracles are more than enough; cease breeding immediately.

(If even 25% of America made these basic, entirely doable cultural adjustments, it would essentially qualify as a revolution...by today's diluted standards.)

"If you are out to describe the truth, leave elegance to the tailor."

—Albert Einstein

What happened after that showdown with the recruiter?

JT: That was an amazing day. We wandered further down 42nd Street until we happened upon a row of street chess players. Their stakes went something like this: If you lose, you pay the guy two bucks. If you win, it's free.

And the coolest part was the giant black dude who stood behind the players and solicited opponents like some kind of goddamned chess pimp. We scrounged up a few bucks and Allie took on one of the "masters" in a speed match.

Now, there's not a whole lot of strategy in blitz chess and that's what these guys were playing. You have to make all your moves in something like three minutes. Allie offered the guy to play the game in one minute and remove one of his pawns—"To make it fair," he said—but the street master foolishly insisted on playing even. The game began.

What amazed me most was Allie's hand movement from the chessboard to the time clock. It was like he knew exactly how far each piece was from the clock. In blitz chess, every second counts and Allie's fluid motion gave him a major league edge. Plus, I just loved to hear him lecture as he played.

"A good opening is vital, but vastly overrated," Allie whispered to his overmatched opponent. "The opening lays the foundation and sets the pace for the middle-game."

His opponent made a tentative move and I noticed a minute

smirk on Allie's face as he aimed a subtle glance in my direction.

"What most people neglect to accept," declared Allie, "is the necessary improvisation of the endgame."

As he spoke the word "endgame," Allie plunked down his bishop and his opponent meekly offering his hand in resignation. I knew what Allie really meant by "endgame," but this poor sap only knew that he had just gotten his chess butt royally kicked.

"You hustling me?" he asked.

"No, I'm just making a point."

"We don't like hustlers, mister."

That was the big black guy, leaning over Allie with fire in his eyes, but I jumped in first.

"How about a simultaneous game?" I asked. "My friend will play all six of your players at the same time, twenty bucks a game. Thirty-minute time limit for all six games..."

A crowd was starting to form now and everyone—except Allie—was energized. He was mellow, as usual.

"Can you afford to lose that much, little man?" The black guy was trying to mock me but I kept my mind on the chess challenge.

"He can wear a blindfold if you want," I taunted.

The games were set up—without the blindfold, of course—and the many on-lookers settled in for a show.

Watching Allie move a piece, slap the clock, and shuffle over to the next table was pure drama. A tour de force, as they say.

Within ten minutes, two men resigned, one was checkmated, and I felt like I was gonna start laughing out loud. With three minutes to go, Allie was down to one opponent—the first guy he had played.

Allie lost some time to gaze at a passing moving van before sitting down across from his rival. The two men moved pieces and struck the clock so quickly that it was impossible to fully understand their strategies.

But, with one minute to go, Allie mated the guy, collected the money, and moved away from the table. The crowd applauded. The black chess pimp nodded in admiration.

A group of college kids from Jersey—even I could pick 'em out a mile away—surrounded Allie.

More from the Internet Insurgent:

Back before it was common to see women and girls playing basketball, I remember seeing two black girls, maybe 13 years old bouncing a basketball while waiting for a train at Lexington Avenue.

They were quite good and were obviously enjoying themselves. Within a few minutes, a white cop came along and admonished them to stop throwing the ball around. The girls frowned and watched him walk away like John Wayne.

One of the girls took the ball and gave it one more toss against the wall.

I may be right or wrong about this but that spirit: making that one last toss against the wall to challenge authority is humanity at its best...

❧

JT: "What are you," one of the kids asked, "some kind of wise homeless guy?"

"Yeah," another one chimed in, "like that *Fisher King* guy."

I just kicked back and grooved on Allie dealing with the concept of "fans." Seven guys and six girls with that holier-than-thou innocence I can laugh at now.

"Tell us something wise," one of the girls asked mockingly. However, she had great lips, I must admit.

"Yeah, chess master," her boyfriend joined in, "teach us something we don't already know."

"Do you have questions?" Allie inquired, and I immediately got out my notebook.

"We're college students," another of the Jersey girls countered. "We have plenty of questions."

That was a pretty good response for a preppie, but Allie eventually cooled her arrogance.

"Give them to me," he suggested. "I'll give them back to you."

"Give them back?" they replied, almost is unison.

"Yes, I'll give your questions back to you with all the answers."

Allie's sudden challenge and his calm, whispery voice unnerved these cocky kids. Slowly, they started asking him chess questions, pushing each other aside for a chance to shout at this strange homeless man.

Allie's face remained exactly the same and his voice never

74

changed pitch or cadence as he easily handled their inquires.

"Surely bright young minds like yours have deeper concerns and queries than some silly game," he whispered. "If this is the best you can do, I must move on. It's getting late."

"But, what do you want us to do?" The loudest of the group, the one with the sweet lips, sounded mighty humble now.

"Each of you," Allie replied, "choose an issue you hold dear and tell it to me. I shall ease your mind. But I want all your subjects to be different; repetition can be so boring." Allie was on a roll. He was sharing some of his vast wisdom.

For the first time, I got the definite feeling that he was realizing that his days were numbered and this message of his had to be heard.

So, thirteen idealistic, indoctrinated youths shouted out their questions, ideas, concerns, and so on—in rapid-fire succession. Allie took it all in like a fuckin' machine.

To these kids, it was like a game...a challenge. The type of challenge they sure weren't getting in their classrooms. Their questions ranged from politics to music to ethics to Old Testament prophecies and beyond. Allie took no notes as he patiently waited for them to finish.

Then, after a subtle breath, he attacked each and every subject on its own and within the context of the other issues. The students were spellbound as Allie spoke without rest, without notes, and without any visible strain.

He spoke in swirling dissertations. When I look at what I jotted down that day, I see lines like this:

"There is one major difference between Democrats and Republicans: they tell different lies to get elected."

"America is a nation built upon myth...and the greatest myth of all is that the land of the free is gonna last forever. I'm sure the Aztecs, the Incas, the Romans, and the Mongols were pretty damn pleased with themselves and figured what they were doing would never end."

"If we don't want our legacy to be one of inaction and shame, we must create drastic, permanent change very, very soon...because here's the most inconvenient truth of all: it's time to embrace a much darker shade of green."

Then, when one of the kids said something about Jesus, Allie delivered this gem:

The Animal Enterprise Terrorism Act of 2006—AETA— specifically targets anyone who "intentionally damages or causes the loss of any real or personal property including animals or records used by animal enterprise, or any real or personal property of a person or entity having a connection to, relationship with, or transactions with an animal enterprise."

Silence...until Allie continued:

John 2:13-16 reads: "In the Temple courts he found men selling cattle, sheep and doves and others sitting at tables exchanging money. So he made a whip out of cords and drove all from the Temple, both sheep and cattle; he scattered the coins of the money changers and overturned their tables. To those who sold doves he said: 'Get out of here.'"

So, you now have an answer for the next time someone asks you "what would Jesus do?" Thanks to the AETA, you can reply: Roughly 12 to 18 months.

He took pleasure in shaking foundations and demolishing what seemed to be secure. His words dazzled these future yuppies and had them suddenly questioning everything they once held as beyond question.

"You talk in a way that makes me wonder about good causes," one guy remarked, his tight shirt clung to his jockish body but he seemed too plastic to be sexual. "Your ideology is so distant," he said.

"Don't get caught up in ideology," Allie warned. "An ideology is as good or as bad as those who embrace it."

"So how can we help people?" The babe who asked that had nice cleavage, but looked like someone who voted for Democrats.

"By understanding yourself," replied Allie as I swore he gazed for one millisecond at her chest. "If it's harmony you seek, aim to change yourself, not only the people around you. You can cover your feet with comfortable shoes but you cannot carpet the world."

"But what about donating money to causes?" Yeah, Ms. Cleavage was most certainly the Sierra Club type.

"What is money?" Allie laughed. "You don't need money to be happy, all you need is something to be enthusiastic about."

"Is that why you live on the street?" Sweet Lips was indignant now.

"Well," responded Allie with a subtle glance toward yours truly, "if you sleep on the street, you needn't worry about falling from your bed."

"But sir," the quietest guy said, "my father is wealthy. Why shouldn't I share in his riches? He owns buildings and all kinds of real estate."

"Your father may own the property," said Allie, growing bored, "but I enjoy the landscape." This quieted them for a bit.

It kinda made me chuckle when the preppies found out how late it was and started to stir.

"Does this mean we break the rules?" inquired the jock with the tight shirt.

"When the situation calls for it."

"How extreme can we get?"

"As MLK said, 'when you're right you can never be too radical.'"

"How can we get started?"

Allie had them sold. When Sweet Lips asked this question, I knew she was ready for revolution.

"That is for you to decide," responded Allie. "Just be aware that growth is attained in degrees but if it is enlightenment you seek, it will come in an instant. You cannot cross the deep chasm in small steps. When the time comes to jump, you best be ready to jump."

I tugged Allie away from his adoring fans. Ms. Cleavage followed us and asked him why he lived on the street and why he wasn't the head of the philosophy department at some university.

I answered that one as we staggered off: "That would be like a fish being the head of the marine biology department..."

Chapter IV from *The Rise of the Pawns*:

How to give a rousing speech

a) Find a quiet place

b) Close your eyes and breathe deeply

c) Think about animals in slaughterhouses and laboratories. Think about humans in prisons. Think about civilians in a war zone. Think about someone you love dying of cancer caused by corporate-created toxins.

d) Give a rousing speech

❧

Did you ever witness Allie writing his Craigslist posts?

JT: Twice. I acted as a lookout of sorts at the public library. I always thought it was amazing that the administrators at Craigslist did not give up the IP address for Allie's insurgent posts.

Why do you suppose they didn't?

JT: A token gesture toward free speech, I guess. Ultimately, if Allie were a genuine threat, they would've found him and shut him down.

Do any genuine threats exist today?

JT: Stay tuned...

Another post by the Internet Insurgent:

In her 1995 book, *Bridge of Courage*, Jennifer Harbury quotes
a Guatemalan freedom fighter named Gabriel, responding to a
plea to embrace non-violent resistance: "In my country child
malnutrition is close to 85 percent," he explains. "Ten percent of
all children will be dead before the age of five, and this is only the
number actually reported to government agencies. Close to 70
percent of our people are functionally illiterate. There is almost
no industry in our country—you need land to survive. Less than
3 percent of our landowners own over 65 percent of our lands.
In the last fifteen years or so, there have been over 150,000
political murders and disappearances... Don't talk to me about
Gandhi; he wouldn't have survived a week here. There was a
peaceful movement for progress here, once. They were crushed.
We were crushed. For Gandhi's method to work, there must be a
government capable of shame. We lack that here."

JT: I noticed that Allie seemed older as we played chess that night. His blue eyes appeared to be sunken deeper into his sad face. The blueness of his eyes hypnotized me, I had never seen anything like them. But he appeared to be aging and getting more frail with each passing hour.

Anyway, he talked endlessly throughout our games. Even after I laid down to sleep, Allie did not stop talking. He told me a lot about the world and a little about himself. When Allie evoked the names of William Blades (the world's top movie star) and Eden (the *enfant terrible* of avant-garde poetry) as his friends and students, I did not completely believe him.

When these two showed up at the Spray Can Prophet's funeral, I felt guilty for harboring any doubts at all about Alphonse Romano.

Allie spoke through the night. He did not sleep. I know this because I woke up several times and heard him in mid-thought. He couldn't have possibly seen my eyes open and began talking that quickly.

His words were profound and disturbing, yet his voice soothed me. I slept to the sound of its steady whisper-like cadence.

His sleepless, talk-filled night gave Allie a ragged look that next day at the bookstand. I manned the chessboard without asking, and stayed there all day except for an hour or so that I spent looking for moving vans.

During that hour, Herbert Mercury took it upon himself to "challenge the chess master." While Allie systematically defeated the corpulent detective, Mercury grilled him about rumors of a chess prodigy loose on the New York streets.

When all he got from Allie was a sermon on the fate of prodigies to accompany the humiliation of being checkmated in fourteen moves, Mercury moved on.

By the time I returned, Allie had put the chessboard away and was giving all his attention to the newspaper in his hand.

"Chess is a foolish expedient for making idle people believe they are doing something very clever when they are only wasting their time."

—G.B. Shaw

Another post by the Internet Insurgent:

We can't give up hope, I'm often told. *Keep hope alive*, the saying goes. *If we lose hope, nothing will ever change...*or so they believe. Well, I'm here to say: *Fuck hope*. We live on a planet brimming with hope yet that same planet is under perpetual assault...and the hopers are losing. The corporations raping our eco-systems don't *hope* they can steal more land, exploit it, poison it, and make boatloads of cash. They make a plan and make it happen...damn the torpedoes. (You might even call it "direct action.")

Monsanto doesn't put its faith in candlelight vigils or humans standing in the shape of a peace sign. They get busy putting their people into positions of power, writing legislation, and bullying and smashing anyone opposed to their insane agenda.

General Motors doesn't reserve its opinions for government sanctioned "free speech zones." The television, Internet, magazines, movies, songs, radio, etc. are all inundated with GM's taxpayer-subsidized propaganda...just as the planet is inundated with GM's output.

McDonald's doesn't waste time *hoping* things will go its way when its days are chock filled with brainwashing, killing, poisoning, destroying...and counting its profits. Hope never enters into the equation.

"Hope is a bad thing," sez Henry Miller. "It means that you are not what you want to be. It means that part of you is dead, if not all of you. It means that you entertain illusions. It's a sort of spiritual clap, I should say."

For most folks, the verb "hope" *is* virtually synonymous with "pray," while "hope" the noun is often interchangeable with "faith."

Hope is for suckers.

JT: Allie told me:

"We have a new mission, my young friend."

"I saw three moving vans today."

"Never mind the moving vans, the endgame is upon us. Tonight, we will embark upon our new objective."

That evening, Allie led his devoted disciple on a sojourn throughout Manhattan, each of us carrying a half-filled can of black paint.

When we first came upon one of his scrawlings, Allie calmly opened his paint can and proceeded to splash its contents on the graffiti poem.

"Fools! I'm a genius, am I? These poems are examples of profound art? I can't allow this to happen!"

I realized then what Allie had seen in the newspaper. The growing notoriety of the Spray Can Prophet had blossomed into full-blown hero worship and the press had deemed his scrawled words to be "art."

Petitions were circulated to protect the graffiti from being removed.

Equally as vociferous was the Spray Can Prophet's opposition. Called everything from a "common criminal" to "the antichrist," Allie found himself the subject of the type of attention he had always shunned. Hence, he felt driven to defile his own work.

When news of the paint attacks on the graffiti poetry hit, the city was gripped in a frenzied backlash. The furor dominated the papers and evening news shows, pushing all details of my disappearance well into the background.

Allie Romano's Reading List

Society of the Spectacle – **Guy Debord**

A People's History of the United States – **Howard Zinn**

Killing Hope – **William Blum**

The Monkey Wrench Gang—**Edward Abbey**

Endgame **(both volumes)** – **Derrick Jensen**

One Minute Wisdom—**Anthony De Mello**

❧

JT: Herbert Mercury was getting nowhere, but my dad was convinced that I was in New York. So, my overweight pursuer pounded the pavement in search of a tiny boy in the midst of eight million other stories.

I later found out that my dad had formulated his theory early. He was following the Spray Can Prophet story and felt sure that I would be enticed by such a figure. So, when Herbert Mercury came back to challenge the chess master, it was propitious that I was again out looking for moving vans.

Mercury took his obligatory beating at chess while he looked over Allie's books.

"These books look awful new, pal." Allie ignored his statement and finished him off in eighteen moves.

The private eye was about to leave when he noticed something that would eventually lead him to me.

The back of Allie's coat was speckled with dark green paint. This sparked Mercury's interest as he recounted my dad's insistence that the Spray Can Prophet figured into this somehow.

He took one last look around the chess master's bookstand and left: he had to double-check that the paint being splashed over the Spray Can Prophet's work was indeed always dark green.

When I returned, it was surprising to see that Allie was packing up for the day. "Alphonse, I saw more moving vans today than ever before. What a busy day. Are you going back to the shack already?"

"Yes, I've decided that our mission is more important than all this."

I never would've guessed that Mercury was following us. Later, I realized that Allie knew, but I had no idea that my father's private detective was prowling around in the shanty while Allie and I covered over the graffiti poems.

Why Allie decided to leave his notebook in the shack that day is just another part of his enigma, and it didn't take long for Herbert Mercury to put two-and-two together and call my dad. At least, I was eventually able to get the notebook back from Mercury.

From Allie's notebook:

Normal means strip malls; normal means strip mining

It means pre-emptive strikes and humanitarian bombing

It means shock and awe

Normal means if you kill someone while wearing a uniform, you get a parade. Do it in gang colors and you get the electric chair.

JT: It was the poem that Allie scrawled on the Vertical Club wall that provoked the commotion. Rush hour was just beginning and our mission had abruptly transformed from covert to overt when Allie splashed mud-black paint over his dark green words. The response might've shocked even him. Then again, probably not...

Another post by the Internet Insurgent:

Voltairine de Cleyre (1866-1912), an American anarchist / feminist writer and theorist, puts it more lyrically: "Every person who ever had a plan to do anything, and went and did it, or who laid his plan before others, and won their co-operation to do it with him, without going to external authorities to please do the thing for them, was a direct actionist. All co-operative experiments are essentially direct action. Every person who ever in his life had a difference with anyone to settle, and went straight to the other persons involved to settle it, either by a peaceable plan or otherwise, was a direct actionist."

"The main object of a revolution is the liberation of man...not the interpretation and application of some transcendental ideology."

—Jean Genet

❧

What are the goals of the Pawns?

JT: I was watching *High Noon* for the billionth time the other night. For me, the most powerful moment in the film is when Amy, the converted Quaker wife (played by Grace Kelly) of Marshal Kane (Gary Cooper) shoots and kills a man to save her husband's life. Earlier in the film, Amy declares: "My father and my brother were killed by guns. They were on the right side but that didn't help them any when the shooting started. My brother was nineteen. I watched him die. That's when I became a Quaker. I don't care who's right or who's wrong. There's got to be some better way for people to live."

However, Amy not only ends up shooting a man, she also fights off the main villain which allows Marshal Kane to finish him off. While *High Noon* was originally created as a McCarthy-era allegory, it stands today as a stark warning not only that the average citizen would rather pretend all is well than stand up and fight but also this: When staring down murderous psychopaths, even pacifists must sometimes choose force. That's what the Pawns are all about.

Can you win? Can we win?

JT: Yes...but winning may simply mean creating a softer place to land.

From Allie's notebook:

Normal means 1 in 31 American adults is in prison, on parole, or on probation but we live in the land of the free

Normal means we carpet bomb civilians from 15,000 feet, label it humanitarianism, and we still live in the home of the brave

Normal means the Department of War was magically transformed into the Defense Department shortly after WWII

Normal: one billion earthlings live on the equivalent of one US dollar a day

❧

JT: I had a front row seat to Allie's suicide.

Suicide?

JT: What else can I call it? He knew he was doomed. I'll tell you what, it's not how I'd do it.

Do what? Commit suicide?

JT: Yeah. If I ever decide to end it all, I'm gonna take as many of them with me as possible.

Can you tell me about the day Allie died?

JT: You gonna put it in your script?

Of course...

JT: The Spray Can Prophet's fans were not pleased by the filthy homeless man who was splashing paint on the graffiti they were fetishizing.

"Hey! That's art you just ruined!"

"What do you think you're doing?"

"Call the cops. This bum just covered our poetry!"

"Don't you know who the Spray Can Prophet is?"

Allie chuckled. "The Spray Can Prophet is a fraud."

The crowd evolved into an angry mob and I found myself shoving people away from my mentor. The sound of approaching sirens chilled me as I tugged on Allie's sleeve.

"Alphonse! We gotta get out of here! C'mon..."

"James!"

It was my father's voice. I froze. Allie turned to stare him down. Mercury was pointing at the homeless man and drawing his pistol as the mob converged violently towards us.

Dad ordered Mercury to rescue me as two cop cars screeched up the curb.

I looked towards Allie as he ducked from the punches of the people he had offended by launching black paint onto his own illegal poetry, the poetry they adored. For some reason, I glanced at my watch: It was 5:15.

"Alphonse, I don't want to go with him."

"The endgame is here for me. No more moving vans. Carry on, my young friend. You take it from here."

Chapter V from *The Rise of the Pawns*:

How to bring down the dominant culture

a) *Ask yourself if you're content with your relatively high quality of life being possible thanks to the poor quality of life of others elsewhere*

b) *Ask yourself if you're content with your relative freedom being possible thanks to the oppression of others elsewhere*

c) *Accept that we are all accomplices to the perpetual global crime called "civilization"*

d) Bring down the dominant culture

JT: As Mercury lifted me off my feet, the cops were trying to rescue Allie from the mob. It was too late. The battered, weakened man couldn't stand up to the punishment.

Men and women in business suits, the same misguided creatures who canonized the graffiti poetry of the Spray Can Prophet—their faces clenched in expressions of alienation and fear—drained the life from Alphonse Romano with their kicks and punches.

My father watched all this closely, carefully monitoring my reaction. He seemed quite aghast at the fact that I did not cry.

In fact, I was smiling.

❧

Do you resent having to give up your promising chess career to use your time defending the planet?

JT: I don't see it that way. This generation is charged with the most critical mission humankind has ever faced—*survival*—and I'd like to imagine Allie would agree that is in indeed the greatest time ever to be an activist. The work we do will impact this planet more profoundly than any previous social movement. When else in all of human history has there been a time when we were in better position to shape the future? We are on the brink of economic, social, and environmental collapse. What a time to be alive.

"The future will only contain what we put into it now"

—Graffiti from May 1968 Paris uprising

"Action is always better than hope. If we don't want our legacy to be one of inaction and shame, we must create drastic, permanent change very, very soon...because here's the most inconvenient truth of all: it's time to embrace a much darker shade of green."

—Alphonse "Allie" Romano

Postscript

A worker at the Indian Point nuclear facility checks his cell phone to see what time it is.

It's 5:14.

You never know...maybe a meteor the size of Namibia will hit in less than one minute.

About the Author

The regular visitors to Mickey Z.'s blog have ordained themselves "The Expendables." Mickey asked them to write a collective bio and here's the result:

"Mickey Z.'s voice is the roundhouse kick of activist literature: profoundly mistrustful of government in all its dreadful guises, while courageously supporting all of us who stand against it. Determined to live the words, rather than simply to speak them, Mickey Z. doesn't get more readers, he just makes more friends. His blog is like a front stoop where we all gather to talk over the news, what's happening with each other, and generally enjoy each other's company. The gentle concern for his fellow humans and the behind-the-scenes acts of kindness are surpassed only by the cuteness of his dimples."

Darker Shade of Green is Mickey Z.'s eleventh book and—unless the laws are changed or the power runs out—he can be found on the web at MickeyZ.net.

Open to any page in *CPR for Dummies* and you just may read a line like this:

He's a priest; of course he hesitated when he realized he was about to hit someone with a crucifix.

OR

I needed to believe someone higher than the government was in charge of things so I went to church.

OR

"We are here to, like, honor your loins and everything," said Ruth.

The world is creeping towards destruction—not theoretically—it's really happening. In these last hours will humanity come together to correct their collective wrongs? Or will there be rampant beatings and kinky sex?

A group of strangers are brought together by synchronicity to answer the age-old question: you lookin' at me, punk? The answer entails the comeuppance of the rich, police brutality, aerobic instruction by the Messiah, sexual slavery, and mutating genes.

(Is this sounding good? I hope so. It's not easy writing these. I'm just a corporate monkey trying to snag your hard-earned dollars but don't let that get in the way of buying this book. Did I mention SEX yet?)

Author Mickey Z's experimental tour-de-force is a funny, challenging deconstruction of the concept of the "novel" as well as life in the United States of America.